Have you Ever...?

Have you Ever...?

Published by Cyan Tayse

Proofreading and Editing by Spell Bound
Cover images from Deposit Photos
Cover design by Inked Imprints

ISBN: 978-0-473-39560-5

Have you Ever...?

A Pocket Rocket Novella

By Cyan Tayse

Chapter One

Cara

"And then he goes, 'you did what with a cucumber?' and I swear to God, Cara, I nearly died!" Brianna hides her face in her hands.

I try not to laugh, really, I do, but when your best friend shares her latest embarrassing story, there really isn't much else you can do. Giggling, I attempt to soothe her by rubbing a hand in circles on her back. "Look on the bright side, at least he now knows you're open to food play," I say with a goofy grin plastered on my face.

"Not helping," she says through her hands. "I have to live with him! I have to see him Every. Damn. Day."

"And that's a bad thing because?" I ask, not seeing the downside at all. He is hot and single; what could possibly be wrong with waking up to that every morning? Catching him in the hall on his way to the bathroom… wearing nothing but those tight boxers, his six pack and delectable V on full display. Mmmmm.

"Seriously, Cara?" The look on her face tells me I have indeed said those things out loud. "Maybe you should hook up with him, then I won't seem like such a freak." She sticks her tongue out at me, her grin returning. That's what I love about her, even when she is amidst a total melt down, she can still find it in her to harass me.

"Maybe I will," I say, snatching a chip from the packet and popping it in my mouth. "I wonder what kind of depraved things I could show him," I mumble around my food.

"I'm sure you could think of something."

Oh, yes, I most definitely could, I think to myself. I've only met him the once, but it was enough to sear his perfection into my brain. I can picture myself climbing up his six-foot frame, wrapping my legs around his tapered waist, while clinging to his broad shoulders. His large hands cupping my ass, rocking me against him as I bite his full bottom lip. God, those lips. I've never seen lips more kissable than his…

"Earth to Cara," Brianna clicks her fingers in front of my face. "You're sex dreaming, aren't you?" She crosses her arms across her chest, pushing her breasts together and giving me an eyeful.

"I'm pleading the fifth," I say, dragging my eyes back up to her face. Brianna and I have been best friends since forever, and never have we stepped over that boundary, though I wouldn't be averse to it. In fact, over the last year, I have often wondered what it would be like to bury my face in those beautiful full breasts of hers. She knows of my passionate trysts with other girls, but I've never had the courage to admit my true feelings to her. Yes, I'm into guys. I like a bit of cock as much as the next girl. But, I also like the soft sensuality of a curvy woman. Men are hot, but women are sexy.

I'm sure Brianna has noticed me checking her out on several occasions, but she's never brought it up, so I haven't either. I wouldn't know what to say anyways. "So, Bri, can I suck your tits?" doesn't really seem like an appropriate thing to say to your best friend.

"You're doing it again! Stop picturing Dan naked, and pay attention to me!" she whines.

Oh, if only she knew the truth.

"Okay, sorry." I hold my hands up in mock surrender. "You have my undivided attention." I put my elbows on my knees and rest my chin on my hands. "What's up, buttercup?"

"You wanna sleep over tonight? Maybe it'll be less awkward if you're there."

"Sure," I say casually. "I'll pack a bag now." Unfolding my legs, I crawl across the bed to grab my bag from behind her, my upper arm brushing past her soft mounds, sending a jolt straight to my centre. I have to stop myself from moaning out loud.

Not wanting to seem like a weirdo, I quickly climb off the bed, and over to my closet. I select my skimpiest shorts and a singlet for sleeping in, along with a summer dress that hugs my curves. I'm not really sure who I want to impress more; Dan or Bri.

Biting my lip, I push the thoughts of the three of us out of my head. That can be a little something I can revisit later, when I don't have an audience.

"All ready," I announce, slinging my bag over my shoulder.

"Great!" She claps her hands gleefully. "You haven't stayed over in so long," she draws out the word 'so' just to drive her point home.

"Yeah, it's been a while," I agree, knowing full well why I hadn't. Seeing Brianna in her day-to-day get up is one thing, but watching her prance around in her satin nightie is quite another. I lick my lips as that image dances in my head.

"You need some chapstick?" she asks, holding some out to me.

"Huh?"

"For your lips. You were licking them, are they dry?"

"Oh, uh, yeah, thanks." I reach forward and accept her offering. "Hey, you wanna grab some drinks, really make a night of it?" I suggest.

"Ooh yes! That will help me compose myself in front of Dan," she says, springing up from her perch on my bed. I swear she still acts as though we are in high school, not nearing thirty.

"Sure it will," I say dryly, one eyebrow raised. "Alcohol is always *my* go-to when I need to feel cool, calm and collected too."

"Shut up and get your ass out the door. We have drinking to do!"

"Yes, Ma'am!" I raise my hand in a salute before sashaying out the door, making sure to add an extra wiggle into my hips.

"Yep, Dan is gonna love you!"

Chapter Two

Dan

"You're full of shit," Evan says, cracking open a beer. "There's no way she said that."

"I'm telling you, man, she honestly did! Scouts honour." I hold up three fingers beside my head.

"Like you were ever a scout," Evan scoffs. "You were probably too busy picking up chicks and getting laid."

I laugh. "You're probably right." Tipping my head back, I let the cool, amber liquid flow down my throat.

"So, you gonna bone her?" Evan waves his hands in front of him to form the shape of a woman before pelvic thrusting.

"What are you? Twelve?" I chuckle. Evan and I met at AMI Stadium last year, when our teams had gone up against each other. I played for the Ravens, and Evan for the Nomads. We bonded over a beer while discussing the ref's decision to yellow-card us both during the game.

I'd been living up in Wellington when I got the offer to join the Nomads down in Christchurch. With a higher salary on the cards, I jumped at the chance. Things had become taxing back home, and I'd been looking for something to spice things up. It couldn't have come at a better time.

Evan had been the first person I'd called. He'd jumped straight in, offering to help me find a flat. Even going so far as to personally check out each and every one while I had tied up loose ends up north. As soon as he'd met Brianna, the sassy red-head with curves in all the right places, he'd known it was the flat for me. I had a bit of a reputation for being a ladies' man. What can I say? My six-foot-five stature, dark hair and piercing blue eyes always pulled them in. What he didn't know though, was that I wasn't one to hook up with flatmates. I knew from personal experience, it never worked out.

"If you're not going to, can I have a crack?" Evan asks, leaning forward in his seat. He is built like a brick shithouse, on the shorter side and stocky. The ladies often refer to him as a teddy bear because of his size. But that's what is to be expected of a tighthead prop.

"Hey, be my guest." I wave my hand around the room. "I don't shit where I eat."

Evan cracks a grin, rubbing his hands together. "Fan-fucking-tastic! With you outta the picture, I might actually have a shot this time." He laughs, shaking his head.

Chapter three

Cara

Popping open a Billy Maverick, I hand it to Brianna before opening one for myself. We opted to walk back to her place so that we could imbibe on our way. She's still packing herself about seeing the six-foot-whatever God that resides in her flat.

When she'd told me she was living with a rugby player, I had thought he'd be just a regular Joe, playing social footy in the evenings. Not some hotshot player who was head hunted to play for the Nomads; the top team in town.

This guy is the real deal. His rock-hard abs are chiselled to perfection, as if carved out of stone. Sure, I'd only had a sneak peek at him while he'd been sauntering down the hall to his room, wearing nothing but a towel, but it had certainly been enough to keep my fingers walking in the dead of night over the last week. Oh yes, I'd catalogued that one under *Spank Bank Number 2*, coming second only to Brianna, of course.

Shoving the remaining cans into my backpack, I sling it over my shoulder once more.

"Thanks again for coming with me," she says, rolling the can across her chest in an attempt to cool down. My eyes are immediately drawn to the tiny droplets of water beading off the can and dripping down her breasts. *Oh, what I wouldn't give to lap that up.* My tongue darts out, catching my lip and pulling it in, my teeth finding purchase. I have to tear my eyes away before I start salivating.

"I still don't see what the problem is. So he thinks you're a perverted sex freak who likes to shove cucumbers up your ass? What of it?" I tease, nudging her with my elbow.

"I didn't shove them up my ass!" she screeches, before slamming her hand across her mouth and looking around to see if anyone heard her. I bark out a laugh.

"*I* know you didn't. But *he* doesn't know that." I love riling her up.

"All I said was that I liked to shove cucumbers into everything. Everything meaning salads and sandwiches, not my ass! And, I was talking to my mum for God's sake! Ewww!" Her green eyes flash, like they always do when she is fired up.

"I think 'shove' may have been your downfall there," I say with a grin. "I don't know about you, but I generally *throw* cucumbers into a salad, not *shove* them."

"Yeah, yeah," she says drily.

"I do *shove* things into my p—"

"Stop!" she interrupts me before I can carry on, her hand darting out to stop my lips from moving. "I don't need to know what you do in your spare time." She rolls her eyes, and I fight the urge to lick her fingers.

I sigh, looping my arm through hers. "Don't lie, you know you live vicariously through my sexcapades."

Giggling, she nods. "You *do* tell the best bedtime stories."

"I really do." I look over at her. "You really should try and experiment a little more. Who knows, maybe you'll like a cucumber shoved up your—"

"Jesus, Cara! If I promise to loosen up, will you stop talking about shoving things in me?"

"It *is* one of my favourite topics of conversation, but I guess I could stop." I reach over and press my finger to the bottom of her can, making her drink. "But first things first, you need to drink more."

***

By the time we reach her house, we are well on our way to being tipsy. Not quite enough for Brianna to be rid of her embarrassment, but tipsy all the same. While she flits back and forth on the porch, trying to build up the courage to go inside, I decide to take charge. Flinging open the door, I announce our arrival. "Honey, we're home!" I holler down the hallway, making a direct line for the bathroom.

"Cara!" Brianna hisses, tailing me. "You can't leave me alone with him!"

Cocking my head to the side, I listen to the voices coming from the lounge. "Good thing he's got someone else here with him then," I say. "Hey, maybe he was just as nervous as you." I smile reassuringly. She, however, doesn't seem convinced. "Look, if you're that worried, just wait here until I'm done."

A smile washes over her face at my words. "Thanks," she mutters, sliding her back down the wall to sit.

Once in the bathroom, I do a quick check of my appearance. Adding a little gloss to my lips, and pushing my hands through my unruly curls, I am happy with what I see. With a spritz of perfume to freshen up after our walk, I step back out into the hall. Reaching down, I grab Brianna's hands and pull her reluctantly to her feet.

"I bet he doesn't even remember." The look she gives me says she thinks that is highly unlikely, but I wave it off. "Who cares what he thinks anyway?" Pulling the box of Mavericks from my bag, I shove them under my arm, while at the same time hurling my bag into her room. "Here," I say, handing her another can. "Drink up, sugarplum." I give her a wink, then with my free hand, I grab her hand and drag her towards the lounge.

Chapter four

Dan

As soon as I hear that voice, my interest is piqued. I recognise those dulcet tones from the brief encounter I shared with Brianna's friend that first night in the flat. I hadn't known anyone was home, so when I'd darted out of the bathroom in just my towel, I'd been caught off guard when the leggy blonde greeted me in the hallway. With her barely-there shorts, and tank top exposing her tanned midriff, the sight of her had stopped me dead in my tracks.

Knowing she is here has my pulse racing. Jumping to my feet, I quickly make my way through to the kitchen for another beer to calm my nerves. Twisting the top off, I pour the cool beverage into my mouth, downing the whole bottle in one go. I brace my hands on the counter. *What's going on here?* I think to myself. *I'm Dan fucking Knight, I don't get nervous around women.*

Shaking my head, I grab another two bottles from the fridge and head back to join Evan in the lounge. "Another?" I ask, handing him the bottle before he can answer.

With a cock of his brow, Evan smirks at me. "That hot, huh?"

"What?" I look at him questioningly.

"Her friend. You've sculled back two beers in two minutes, and I saw the look on your face when you heard her voice." He finishes his beer with a sigh, placing the empty bottle on the table and reaching for the next one.

"What look?" I scoff, taking a seat on the couch, one arm draped across the back. "I don't know what you're talking about."

"Pfft, whatever, man. You like her."

Before I can retort, the hot-as-fuck blonde steps into the room, dragging Brianna behind her. "Hello, boys," she says, drawing out the words with a sly wink. "I see we've got some catching up to do." She nods at the empties lined up on the table. "Good thing we brought these." She unceremoniously slaps the box of bourbons down on the table, throwing herself down on the couch beside me. With one leg tucked beneath her, she leans into me with her arm extended. "I don't think we've been properly introduced. I'm Cara McNally. You must be Dan?"

I take her hand in mine, her silky-smooth skin feels like heaven, and I can't help but wonder what it would feel like wrapped around my cock. Clearing my throat, I sit forward, hoping to hide my arising arousal at just the touch of her hand. *Get a grip, Dan!*

"That's me. Nice to meet you, Cara," I manage to say. Waving my hand to the side, I quickly add, "This here is Evan Rider, tighthead prop for the Nomads."

"Ah, so you're the lovable rogue that Bri was telling me about," she says as she casts her eyes over him.

"Cara!" Brianna cries out in embarrassment.

Evan's eyes light up. He turns to Brianna, who is hiding her face. "You think I'm lovable?" A shit-eating grin spreads across his face.

"Oh yeah, she couldn't stop talking about you after you came by." Cara winks.

"Stop!" Brianna hisses at her friend, her face turning a lovely shade of red.

"There's nothing to be embarrassed about. He's loving it, aren't you Ev?" This girl is something else. She oozes confidence like no other. She is definitely someone who is comfortable in her own skin, and rightfully so. She's only been in the room for a few minutes, and already my eyes have canvassed her form, taking in her gentle curves. She is a little more covered up than the last time I saw her, but then again, so am I. Her tight-fitting jeans hug her body, and the low-cut singlet she is wearing, gives me the perfect view of her full breasts. When I lift my eyes, I am surprised to see her smirking at me, as she catches me checking her out. Without taking her eyes from mine, she brings her drink to her lips, her tongue darting out before taking a sip, and all I can think about is how much I want to be that can.

"When you're done eye-fucking over there," Evan starts, reminding me that we have company, "You wanna play a little Never Have I Ever? Get to know each other a little better?" He waggles his eyebrows, making the girls laugh. A quick glance tells me that Brianna has gotten over her embarrassment and is now perched on the chair opposite Evan.

"I'm game if you are," Cara says, with a look that says *I dare you.*

Nobody challenges Dan Knight. "Challenge accepted."

Chapter Five

Cara

"Never have I ever… had a threesome." Evan sits back with a smirk, his legs stretched out in front of him.

"Wow, just going straight into the juicy stuff, huh?" I've barely had a chance to put my drink down. Knowing the boys both have their eyes glued to my every move, I slowly bring the can back up to my lips, lapping up the drops on the edge of the can, before swallowing back another mouthful.

Evan coughs uncomfortably, muttering something under his breath as he adjusts himself. "So… ah…" His face flushes as he tries to get his mouth around the words. "I gotta ask…" He cocks an eyebrow at me, and I know what his question is going to be before he even says a word.

"Two girls, one guy." I turn to Brianna with a grin, tipping my drink in her direction. "I believe it's your turn."

"Hold up! What was that look? You mean…" he points back and forth from Brianna to me. "You two…"

Dan sits forward in his seat. "You two have made out?"

I look at Brianna and without missing a beat, she stares Evan straight in the eye and says, "Oh yeah, sure. All the time. Ya know, when we're running around in our knickers having pillow fights." The sarcasm runs deep with this one.

A defeated look crosses Evan's face. "So, that's a no, then?"

"Why? Are you trying to tell us something?" I quirk my brow. "Have *you two* hooked up?" I gasp and hold my hand to my chest in mock surprise.

"What? No, of course not." Evan coughs and quickly sits back, finishing his can. Dan smirks at his friend's reaction. Interesting.

After a beat, I turn back to Brianna who is clearly amused at the goings on. "Never have you ever..?" I prompt. We'd played this game many a time before, and somehow, I always ended up drinking the most, and divulging my every secret. Brianna, on the other hand, hasn't been quite so experimental – or so she'd have people believe. She always manages to turn the tables on everyone else.

"Never have I ever…" She looks at me with a devilish grin. Oh God, here it comes. "Streaked at a rugby game."

"No." The word is said on a whisper of a breath as both Dan and Evan turn back to me, waiting to see my confirmation.

"It was once, and I was dared," I say, sculling back the last of my can. I point my empty at Bri with narrowed eyes. "You promised."

"I'm sorry," she says through her laughter. "It was just too good not to! I promise this is the last time I bring it up." She crosses her finger across her chest then blows me a kiss. With that cute grin of hers, and that sparkle in her eye, how could I stay mad?

"Wait, are you?" Evan slaps the back of his hand into Dan's chest. "It's her! She's the Blonde Bullet!" He throws his head back in a raucous laugh. "I can't believe I didn't recognise you!"

"Well, I do have all my clothes on, so there's that…"

Folding his arms across his perfectly formed chest, Dan lets out a low whistle. "Normally we'd frown upon things like that, but even I have to admit, that was pretty impressive. I mean, it's not often that a woman… and the speed!" He shakes his head at the memory. "Those fat bastards never saw you coming." He chuckles.

Cupping his hand around his mouth, Evan imitates the commentators' voices, "And now the ball's with Grigg, he runs across field and passes to Tokomo, he takes the tackle and he loses the ball forward! The play breaks down and the ref calls knock-on…" He pauses, turning to Dan as if he's the second commentator in the box. "Well, Smithy, we haven't seen this for a while! A break-down in play and some idiot's decided to make a spectacle of themselves and streak across the field! I don't believe it! This makes a pleasant change, it's actually a woman!"

Dan jumps to his feet, unable to help himself. He holds his bottle up to his mouth like a microphone, and places his hand over his ear as if wearing an earpiece. "I wonder if they'll actually tackle her. Oh, here we go! The security guys are after her! They're having trouble catching up, she's across the centre of the field and almost at the far touch line!"

"Ya reckon they'll get her, Smithy?"

"I dunno, she's pretty speedy. She'd make a good winger, wouldn't ya say, Jono?"

"Yeah I reckon she'd give Usain Bolt a run for his money!"

Pointing across the room, Dan speaks excitedly into his make-shift mic. "Look, she's made it over the sponsors' signs... and... and... what's she doing now, Jono?"

"She's tipping her hat at the crowd!" Evan begins to laugh, an over-the-top, fake, belly laugh. "And she's off into the crowded grandstand!"

"Oh, they'll never catch her now!"

The boys collapse back onto their chairs, holding their stomachs as they snigger.

"Yuck it up, boys." I commend them with a slow clap. "That's super impressive how you remember that word for word. Quite a talent you have there."

"Are you kidding? That's seared into my brain! That shit never happens anymore!" Evan shuffles forward in his seat, resting his elbows on his knees. "I just have one question."

Reaching forward, I pull another can from the box and flick it open, taking a sip before answering him. "Ask away." I wave my hand in front of me as if to say, I'm an open book.

"How did you get out without being caught? I mean," he lowers his voice, "you were naked."

"Except for her hat," Brianna pipes up.

I tip my drink towards her once more. "Yes, we can't forget the hat." No matter how many times she makes me rehash this story, it never seems to get old with her. I can't help but grin back at her. "I might have had a little help at the other end."

"You were there?" Evan asks her, his eyes shining with amusement.

"Of course! What kind of friend would I be if I'd left her in all her naked glory? It was the least I could do… after daring her in the first place." She grins, taking a swig of her drink.

"*You* dared her?" A deep laugh bursts from his chest. "That's the best thing I've heard all year!"

"Did they ever find out who you were?" Dan asks, angling his body towards me.

"Nope. The crowd closed around me, shielding me from security while I dressed." I lean into him. "It may not have been my smartest moment, but damn if it wasn't exhilarating. All those eyes on me." I run my hand down my neck, over my breasts and down to my thighs. "What a rush!"

Chapter Six

Dan

This girl will be the death of me. With her hands roaming her body, she flashes me the most devilish grin, and my cock jumps to attention. I can't tell if she is playing with me, or if she is actually interested. Either way, I am hooked.

"You make it very hard to concentrate when you do things like that."

"I can see that." Her eyes flick down to the bulge in my pants and back up, one side of her mouth pulled up in a sexy-as-hell, lop-sided grin. "Guys are so easy." She pulls back, chuckling lightly.

Yep, she's fucking with me. Damn.

"Must be my turn, right?" She taps her finger against her chin. "What to choose, what to choose?" She peers around the room as if looking for inspiration.

"Shit, is there anything she hasn't done?" Evan asks Brianna, who is helping herself to another drink.

"Mmm." She looks up to the ceiling, considering his question. Her wavy red hair sways side-to-side as she shakes her head. "Not a lot, no."

"Never have I ever… done a body shot."

"I find that hard to believe." Evan sniggers, taking a large gulp of his drink. "How has someone who's had a threesome and streaked in public, never done a body shot?"

"I don't know." She shrugs. "I guess it's just never come up."

"Well, we'll have to rectify that then, won't we?" I jump to my feet, making my way into the kitchen. After opening and closing several cupboards and coming up empty, I peer back around the door. "Where do we keep the shot glasses, Bri?"

"In the cupboard above the bench. There might even be some tequila in there." *Thank you, Evan. You really outdid yourself when you found this place.*

With four shot glasses and a lime in one hand, and a bottle of tequila and the salt shaker in the other, I join the group in the lounge. I pour four full shots of tequila, and slice the lime into quarters. "So, I noticed you didn't drink either, Bri. Evan and I have both done our fair share of these when out celebrating with the boys." I point at the shots lined up on the table. "Two shots each. One off each other, and one off us." I fold my arms across my chest, pleased I've come up with such a clever idea.

"Oh, it's like that, is it?" Cara licks her lips. "I think I can manage that." She turns to

Brianna with a cock of her brow. "You up for it?"

With a few drinks under her belt now, she is quick to nod her agreement. "Sure."

"You wanna go first?" Cara asks, grabbing a lime wedge and placing it in her mouth.

"Okay." Brianna shrugs. She swipes a shot from the table and pushes it in between Cara's breasts.

"Really *shove* it in there," Cara says around the lime. She has a smirk on her face and I can only assume that she knows what I overheard, as I watch a blush creep its way up Brianna's neck and face.

"Okay, here goes." She huffs out a breath before lowering her face to Cara's chest. She tentatively licks just above the edge of her top. She pulls back and sprinkles salt over the wetness. Peering up at her friend, she gives a little sigh before going back in, lapping up the salt, then clasping her teeth around the glass. She pulls it from its resting place and shoots it back. The glass falls from her lips, into her hand, and then Evan and I watch with our mouths hanging open, as her lips move in to Cara's. Their lips barely brush each other as she pulls the lime out of her mouth, but it is enough to redden Brianna's cheeks again. Even Cara has a bit of colour showing, and that is what really intrigues me. *Does she have a thing for her best friend?*

"Yeaow!" Evan calls out, clapping his hands. "That was hot!" He quickly moves to an empty space in the room and lies down, pulling his shirt up. "Now, you gotta take a shot off me." He winks as he places his hands behind his head, eliciting a giggle out of Brianna.

"Um, how do I…?" She stands, staring at his body with her hands on her hips.

"Here, you put the shot in his belly-button." Cara balances the shot glass gingerly. "Try not to move," she whispers to Evan. She licks a trail up his middle and sprinkles the salt on. "He's all yours."

Bri straddles Evan, her hands braced on his hips as she leans forward and runs her tongue along the same path Cara's had been.

Evan groans under his breath, and Cara and I exchange a look before bursting out laughing.

Tequila begins to trickle down his sides as he shoots a look at us, which only makes us laugh harder. Brianna quickly laps up the tequila and fastening her teeth around the glass once more, she throws her head back, letting it flow down her throat.

When she's done, she spits the glass across the floor, and slowly creeps up his body, latching onto the lime. Evan's hands automatically wrap around her, pulling her against him. She giggles as she pulls away, triumphant. She holds the lime in the air. "I did it! Now, it's your turn."

Chapter seven

Cara

This is it. Over the last year, I've dreamed of this moment. Well, maybe not this exact moment, but close enough. I am about to get up close and personal with my best friend.

Brianna stands before me, her chest pushed out, waiting for me to place the shot glass between her gorgeously soft mounds. I lick my lips, stepping in close. "You ready?" I breathe. *Geez, Cara, get a grip.*

"As I'll ever be." She giggles, making those delicious bags of fun jiggle about. I suppress another groan as I ever-so-gently push the shot glass deep into her cleavage. My heart thumps in my chest as I place the lime wedge between her full lips. I trail my finger down her jaw with a wink, letting her think I'm playing it up for the boys' benefit.

Darting my tongue out to moisten my lips once more, I duck my head under her chin, licking a long trail from where the shot glass rests, nestled deep between her breasts, to the outer edge where her top begins. I run my tongue from there up to the base of her neck, forming an arc with my tongue. Her sharp intake of breath spurs me on. I grab the salt and sprinkle a little over my trail before diving back in to lap it all up. I can feel her heart racing as I take my time, a grin spreading across my face as I realise she is just as turned on as I am.

Burying my face between her breasts, I latch onto the shot glass and with a gentle shake of my head, and her silky-smooth skin brushing against my cheeks, I pull the glass up and out, tipping my head back. I let the cup fall into my hand and stepping forward, I grab a hold of her hip, pulling her into me as I tilt my head towards hers. I run my tongue along her bottom lip before securing my mouth around the lime, our lips brushing against each other.

When I pull back, her eyes are closed and her breath is coming out in pants. Slowly, she blinks them open, her heated gaze meets mine and I know in this moment, she wants me too.

Before I have a chance to react, Evan clears his throat, breaking the spell. “Damn girl! That was hot!” He’s still lying across the floor, his hands now clasped in front of him, covering what I’m sure is a raging hard-on.

When I turn back to Brianna, her cheeks are flushed and she won’t meet my eyes. *Damn it, Evan!*

“It was just a bit of fun,” she murmurs, as if trying to convince herself. She keeps her eyes down, staring at a spot on the floor.

Look at me, damn it. It was more than just a bit of fun to me.

"So, ah, I guess it's my turn then." Dan steps forward, offering me the last remaining shot glass. "Where do you want me?"

With one last look at Brianna, I plaster a smile on my face, turning to face Dan. "Wherever you wanna be." I give him a playful shove towards the couch. Gripping the hem of his jersey, he quickly whips both his tops off, giving me a perfect view of his six pack. I am impressed, really, I am. But, he is no Brianna.

Once he is on his back, I place the shot glass on his belly, as I had with Evan. Reaching for the salt, I bring my eyes up to Bri's, hoping to see a hint of that flame again, but all I see is confusion. With a sigh, I turn my attention back to the body before me. Knowing they are waiting for a show, I get down on my knees and leaning over his body, I slowly lick along his stomach, just above the top of his pants, following the treasure trail up to his navel. This should be hot, but all I can think about is the look on her face. It feels wrong to be doing this after what we just shared, even if it was a fleeting moment.

I quickly down the shot of tequila and crawl my way up to his mouth, the lime firmly between his teeth. When I hover above him, his hands go around the back of my neck, pulling me down to meet his mouth. He lets go of the lime wedge just before our lips meet. This is a move I have been known to pull, so it shouldn't surprise me as much as it does. I pull back as soon as I realise what he is doing, but not until after it is too late. I'd kissed him back, albeit briefly.

Shit.

Brianna sits there, almost as stunned as I am. She has her hand to her chest, her eyes wide and fixed on the scene before her. *God, I'd give anything to know what she is thinking.*

Chapter eight

Brianna

What the hell just happened? The single hottest moment of my life just played out, that's what. Sure, I've noticed her looking at me before, but I'd thought it was just like when I check out guys; it doesn't mean anything. But the way she dragged her tongue along my skin… I've never felt anything so electric before. I had to stop myself from throwing my arms around her and slamming my lips to hers.

Where those thoughts came from, I have no idea. I'd never once considered hooking up with a girl before, but damn if I don't want to throw myself at her right now. The only thing is, it was all just an act. I saw her wink, I knew it was all to see how flustered she could make the guys. And boy did it work, if Evan's boner is anything to go by. I just wish it hadn't worked so well on me.

Watching her trail her tongue along Dan's rippled muscles, it is clear to me what her feelings are. I mean, how could I possibly compete with Dan fucking Knight? The star athlete and epitome of all things sexy. The answer is simple. I can't.

Chapter nine

Dan

Wow. Her lips are even softer than I imagined them to be. I hadn't planned on kissing her, but when she dragged her tongue along my skin, a spark was ignited inside and I couldn't help myself. I'd hoped it would last a little longer than it had, but beggars can't be choosers, and I'll take anything she is offering.

As she pulls away from me, her eyes dart over to Brianna, knocking the wind out of my sails. I'd seen the way they'd looked at each other, I'm not stupid. There is definitely something between them, even if they haven't realised it yet. I guess I'd just hoped that her flirtation meant more than just that.

That was a shit move, Dan. It was just meant to be a bit of fun.

I sit up, grabbing my jersey and throwing it back on. "So, ah, whose turn is it?" I ask, knowing full well that it is mine.

Brianna seems to snap out of her daze at my words. She leans forward in her seat, snaffling another bourbon from the table. "I believe it's yours," she says with a smile.

"Oh, this should be good," Evan says, pulling himself up off the floor. "Dan here is a bit like you, Cara. He's done all kinds of crazy shit." He grins, waving an empty bottle in the air. "Another one?"

"Yeah, man, that'd be great, thanks."

"You want a hand?" Brianna asks, jumping to her feet and following him through to the other room.

Cara tucks her legs up underneath her again, toying with the tab on her can.

I feel like such a shithead. "Hey," I say, placing a hand on her arm. "I'm sorry. I shouldn't have done that."

"Don't worry about it." She waves her hand dismissively. "We're here to have a good time, aren't we?"

"Okay, sure. So, we're good?"

"Yeah, of course." She smiles, stretching one of her feet towards me, giving me a little kick. "Stop being such a girl."

"Evan!" Brianna giggles as she saunters back into the room, her face flushed, holding a bowl of chips in her hand. Evan trails behind, his arms loaded with booze, and his eyes fixed firmly on her ass.

With my hand still on her arm, I feel Cara stiffen briefly before she regains her composure. "Took you long enough," she jokes, helping herself to a handful of chips. "Mmmm, salt and vinegar, my favourite." Her words are muffled by the mouthful of chips she's shovelled in there. And somehow, I still find her sexy. Go figure.

After unloading his haul on the table, Evan grabs two stubbies, popping the tops off both before handing one to me. "What's it gonna be?"

"Yeah, Dan, what have you never done?" Cara asks, shuffling closer. "Mr All Kinds of Crazy Shit, I bet you can't think of anything."

I lean in as if divulging something juicy. "I'll let you in on a little secret. Evan doesn't know jack shit." She chuckles at my confession and the sound is like music to my ears. Who cares if she was making eyes at her best friend, *I* made her laugh. And I am determined to make it happen again. At least I was, until the next words slip from my mouth, "Okay, I've got one. Never have I ever, used vegetables in the bedroom." I sit back, instantly feeling like an asshole as soon as I say it. Brianna's eyes snap up to mine, her cheeks flaming red. She looks from me to Evan, to Cara and back again.

Why did you say that? You're supposed to be winning Cara over, not embarrassing her friend.

"What are you? Some kind of prude?" Cara asks, taking a big swig of her drink. I don't miss the wink she sends Bri's way. "Who hasn't spiced things up in the bedroom with a bit of fruit and veggie action?"

"Yeah, Dan." Evan back-hands me in the chest. "You gotta spice things up a bit, bro." He grins at Brianna, waggling his eyebrows at her. "Wouldn't you agree, Bri?"

"Nothing like a carrot up your jacksie," Cara adds, grabbing another handful of chips as if this is an everyday conversation. "Or a firm banana."

"God, Cara! A banana? Wouldn't that get all squishy?" Brianna is in hysterics listening to her friend come to her rescue. I have to admit though, there is something sexy about a woman who isn't afraid to out herself to ease her friend's embarrassment.

"Yeah, that's why it's gotta be a firm one, ya know, still a bit green. Believe me, you do *not* want to clean mashed banana out of your vajayjay."

I nearly spit my drink clear across the room with that one. The way she said it was so blasé. Like she just doesn't care what people think. And you know what? It only makes me want her more.

Chapter ten

Cara

Crisis averted. Brianna is giggling again, her cucumber debacle forgotten about. Who cares if Dan and Evan think I'm a freak? I certainly couldn't give two shits. All that really matters to me, is that Bri is happy. Nothing makes my heart sing more than that cute grin she has. The one that makes her eyes sparkle and her dimples pop. Not to mention the way her laughter makes her breasts bounce. *God, she's sexy.*

"Cara, you're one of a kind, that's for sure." Evan chuckles. "Where did you find her?" He hooks his thumb in my direction as he takes a hefty swig of his drink.

Brianna's eyes land on mine and the greens shine brightly as her lips curl into a grin. "Hanging upside down with her knickers on display."

"Pppppttttt," Evan's mouthful of beer comes spewing out of his mouth and across the table.

"Dude! The chips!" I make a dive for the bowl, trying to protect my precious chips from his spray.

"Sorry." He coughs, thumping his fist into his chest as he chokes on the liquid that is already halfway down his throat. "That was not what I expected you to say." His voice sounds strained, as if he is fighting back another cough.

"You good?" I ask, sitting back and bringing the chip bowl with me. I don't care who you are, you do *not* waste chips, especially salt and vinegar ones! I give the bowl a quick inspection to make sure there are no casualties. Holding one up I declare, "Nobody panic! The chips are still good!"

Dan's deep chuckle rumbles beside me and my lady parts make an involuntary quiver. I can't seem to keep up with myself. One minute I'm pining for Brianna, the next I'm ready to jump Dan's bones. Decisions, decisions. Whatever is a girl to do?

"So, is that true?" He turns to me, flashing that boyish grin of his.

"That the chips are still good? Sure." I toss one into my mouth to prove it.

"Excellent," he says, reaching for the bowl. "That's not what I meant though." He snaffles a handful, keeping his eyes on me, waiting for an admission of guilt.

With a sigh, I pull my leg up, resting my heel on the edge of the couch, the bowl now resting between us. "Yes, I may have been upside down with my knickers on display, but in my defence, I was eight and we were on the monkey bars at school."

"Well played," Evan says with an imaginary tip of his hat to Brianna.

"She loves it really."

"Mmmm, yes, tis true. I love to be the only one who has their laundry aired for all to see. Such fun!" She's right though, I have never been one to shy away from the limelight. What can I say? I like an audience. I swear I missed my calling. I should've been an actress or something. All this confidence, and nowhere to unleash it. "I can't be the only interesting one here. Surely you two have done something outrageous. I mean, you *are* world famous in New Zealand." I wink at Brianna as I reach across the table to retrieve another drink, making sure to give her an eyeful of the goods.

Dan scoffs. "World famous in New Zealand, eh? I think you'll find we're known abroad as well." He huffs on his nails and brushes them against his shirt, a smirk playing across his face.

"Too right!" Evan stands up, emptying the last of his drink into his mouth before adding it to the others lined on the table. "*Everyone's* heard of the Nomads." He looks at me pointedly. "World famous in New Zealand," he mutters with a shake of his head.

He squeezes past Brianna's knees, making sure to rub his hand across her lap as he does. A tinge of pink trails up her neck, giving her cheeks a rosy colour, and she looks down at her feet submissively. There is something so adorable about the way she reacts to attention from anyone who shows an interest. Of course, I'd prefer that it was me making her blush that way, especially after having a taste of what she has to offer.

My mouth begins to water as I recall the creamy flesh I had my lips on not so long ago. A deep throbbing in my core is getting me hot under the collar, and I have to lift my hair off my neck, to cool down a little. Brianna's eyes are locked on mine, watching my every move, her lips parted, and all I can think about is how it would feel to slide my tongue between those lips.

Dan coughs uncomfortably beside me as he shifts in his seat, drawing her attention away. Her blush deepens and she searches the room for anything to look at but me.

Evan returns from the bathroom, stopping abruptly in the doorway, his eyes swinging back and forth between the three of us. “Woah, what did I miss?” When nobody answers, he simply shrugs and grabs himself another beer. “Must be my turn then, huh?”

“Sure is.” Brianna reaches her hand out, those gentle fingers of hers brushing against his thigh as he walks past her. “What have you got for us?”

Envy courses through my body as I watch her stroke him tenderly. I know she felt the connection we had, but obviously she’s not ready to deal with it yet. Fine. Two can play at that game.

Scooting closer to Dan, I lift my legs up and over his, taking his hand and placing it on top of my thigh. If my actions surprise him, he doesn’t show it. “Yeah, Evan, do your worst.” I stick my tongue out at him in a childish manner, unable to contain the jealousy streaking through my veins.

“Right then.” He looks at me with one eyebrow raised. “Never have I ever…”

Chapter eleven

Dan

Don't say it, please don't say it.

"… been in love with my best friend."

Shit, he fucking said it.

All eyes are on Cara, waiting for her to confess her feelings for Brianna, so I do what any guy trying to get his dick wet does; I fucking take a sip of my beer, don't I? As expected, those eyes all turn on me, eager for me to dish the dirt. Of all the things that could have come up in this godforsaken game, this is the one I never wanted to relive, yet here I am, about to spill my guts.

"Let's get this over with," I say, leaning back in my seat. "What do you want to know?" Out of the corner of my eye, I watch as Cara takes a sip of her drink, surreptitiously admitting her guilt alongside me. I know the other two are too preoccupied with me to notice, but I don't draw attention to it.

"Everything. We want to know everything." Evan watches me, as if waiting for me to admit that I'm making it all up. If only that were true.

"Yeah, who was she?" Brianna asks gently, sensing my unease.

"Her name was Nikki, and we'd been friends for ten years. Her family moved in next door to us when we were twelve. She was this crazy tom-boy who liked to climb trees and ride bikes, like me. We'd bike to and from school together every day, and spend our weekends exploring the neighbourhood."

"She sounds like fun," Cara says, wiggling further down the couch so that she can hook her legs over the edge, her ass pushed up against my thigh. My hand drops back down to rest on her leg, just above her knee.

"She really was. We did everything together." My eyes glaze over as I take another swig of my drink. "It wasn't until she got her first boyfriend that I realised how I felt about her. The guy was a prick, used to treat her like shit. If it wouldn't have upset her, I'd have knocked some sense into him." Without meaning to, my grip on Cara's thigh tightens and she lets out a tiny gasp. "Sorry," I whisper, caressing the tender spot.

"So, what happened? Did she leave him?" Brianna is perched on the edge of her seat, her eyes boring holes into mine.

"Yeah, eventually. After that, I took it upon myself to be her protector. Word spread that anyone who hurt her would have me to deal with. I was in the first fifteen by then, and had packed on quite a bit of muscle. No one would go near her."

"You cock-blocked her?"

"Yeah, I guess I did." I chuckle, raking my hand through my hair. "Anyway, when school finished, we went flatting together.

One night, after a few drinks, she broke down in tears, asking me what was wrong with her that no guy would go near her. I felt like a right shit, but I couldn't admit to her that it was my fault, so I just held her as she cried. When she looked up at me with those big eyes full of pain, I couldn't help it. I kissed her." Brianna gasps and Evan makes a fist pump in the air. "She kissed me back and well, you probably know what happened next."

"You got it on," Evan sings in a poor attempt at a Marvin Gaye impression, wiggling his hips suggestively.

"Evan!" Brianna says, slapping his leg playfully. "They made love. He was in love with her." With her elbow resting on her knee, she drops her chin into her palm, turning back to me with a dreamy look in her eyes. "Was it everything you'd hoped it would be?"

"No." I shake my head. "It was so much better than I'd ever imagined it could be."

"So, you became a couple?"

"For two blissful days, yes."

"What happened?"

"One of the boys came by, saw us together. I'd heard he'd had a thing for her, but I never expected him to react the way he did."

"He punched you, didn't he?" Evan doesn't know the story, so I shouldn't be mad at him for saying it so lightly, but my jaw clenches tight all the same. As if she can read my mind, Cara's cool hand lands on mine, her thumb drawing slow circles, giving me something else to focus on.

"He confronted me, made sure she heard about how I'd scared everyone away from her. The hurt in her eyes… I couldn't bear to see it." An image of her grey eyes clouded with tears flashes in my mind. "I told him to leave but he refused, kept pushing me. He swung, but I saw it coming and ducked. I didn't know she was standing behind me."

I train my eyes on Cara's hand, knowing that if I make eye-contact with anyone right now, I won't be able to stop the tears. "She flew backwards, landed on the glass coffee table…"

"It's okay, Dan, you don't have to keep going." Cara sits up and wraps herself around me, her chin resting on my shoulder. "I'm so sorry," she whispers, rubbing her hand up and down my arm.

"Shit... I... fuck, I'm sorry, man, I had no idea." I can hear Evan speaking, but can't bring myself to acknowledge him. "I didn't know..." I feel more than see them get up and leave, the door closing softly behind them, their hushed voices echoing in the hall.

"You okay?" Cara asks. "Anything I can do?"

I shake my head. "I feel like such an ass. I never meant to get into it like that. What a downer, huh?"

"Weeeelllllll," she draws the word out, a grin playing across her face. "I mean, I didn't wanna say anything..." I nudge her with my elbow and she responds by hugging me tight. "You're not so bad."

"Gee, thanks."

She pulls back, staring into my eyes. "You don't fool me, ya know? I know why you did it."

"Did what?" I ask.

"Took the fall for me." I start to protest, but she shushes me with a finger to my lips. "Thank you."

Chapter twelve

Cara

With my finger pressed to his lips, and my arms still wrapped around his shoulders, I am in the perfect position to kiss him if I want to. The only thing is, he knows about my feelings for Brianna, that's the only reason he jumped on in there and saved me with his devastatingly sad story. I can't exactly jump him now; that would be in poor taste. *Oh, sorry your ex got all mangled, but thanks for saving me back there, you wanna make out?*

Somehow it doesn't seem like the appropriate thing to say in this situation.

There goes that plan, I guess. Not only have I made Brianna uncomfortable, sending her fleeing into Evan's arms, but I've single-handedly cock-blocked myself with Dan. Guess I packed my skimpy clothes for nothing.

A cough outside the door reminds me that Evan and Brianna made themselves scarce. "You good? Can our friends come back to play?" I ask, my lips pushed into an over-the-top pout, duck-face, if you will. Whatever you want to call it, it has the desired effect. Dan's grin spreads across his face as he lifts one of his fingers to flap up and down on my lips. I hum against his fingers, the sound reverberating. Oh yeah, we are back in business. "It's okay, guys. You can come back in now," I call.

When Evan pokes his head around the door, I give a quick nod to let him know everything is all good. "Shit, man, I'm really—"

"Ut!" I interrupt him with my hand in the air. "Not another word, everything's easy breezy up in here, right, Dan?" I bend my arm, resting it on his shoulder as I wait for him to answer.

"Like Sunday morning," he says with a wink, and I find myself snorting out a laugh. I knew there was a reason I liked this guy. "She gets me." He points his thumb over his shoulder at me.

"Anyone who doesn't should be ashamed. Seriously, that shit was gold right there."

"Damn right it was, Lionel, my man." Evan raises his palm to slap down onto Dan's in appreciation. "So, we still drinkin'?" He sits back down, popping the cap off his next bottle of beer and placing another on the table in front of them. "I grabbed you one just in case."

"Cheers." They clink their bottles together before taking a swig. "You guys still up for playing, or did I ruin it for everyone?"

"I'm in if you are." I let my hand slap down on his chest. Brianna's tiny hand is engulfed in Evan's with no look of moving. They exchange a look, as if needing to drive the point home some more before answering with a nod.

"Hell yeah, I'm in." With a tug of his hand, Evan pulls her to sit on his lap. Not that I can complain, I'm practically sitting in Dan's lap myself, but I am past the point of caring. Brianna has made her point loud and clear. I should never have got my hopes up like that. The entire time we've been friends, she's never once suggested that she might be interested in trying a *taste of the peach.*

"Must be your turn then, Bri." Lifting my foot, I poke my toe into her knee. "You think of anything while you were out there, or were you two too busy getting busy?" My hips rotate in some form of distorted pelvic thrust while I simultaneously pull a sex face. Yeah, I'm that girl.

"Cara!" Bri giggles, grabbing a handful of chips and throwing them at me.

"What?" Placing my hand against my chest, I feign shock. "You mean you haven't… you're a…?" I gasp.

"Shut up!"

"Wait, are you for real?" The look on Evan's face is priceless as he almost salivates over the prospect of being her first.

"No!" we both chorus before erupting into a fit of giggles. "Sorry to burst your bubble there, mate. Bri's been around the block a few times. And then some!"

"Cara!" She turns to face Evan, trying to keep a straight face. "She's lying. I mean, about being around the block a few times. I'm not *that* easy."

I put the can to my lips before saying, "She ain't no nun either."

"Stop, you're gonna get me in trouble." She giggles again, and even though I know I am setting myself up for disappointment, I still revel in the fact that I am the one making her laugh.

"Oh pssh," I wave my hand flippantly, "like he's all sweet and innocent." I aim my can at Evan.

"Wouldn't you like to know." He waggles his eyebrows at me while slurping back another mouthful of beer.

"Nope, not really," I say with a straight face. God I love fucking with people, and Evan makes it all too easy. "I've never been interested in sloppy seconds." I wink and watch as his brows shoot up as high as they possibly can.

"Oh my God, Cara!" She turns to Evan, her cheeks flaming red. "Ignore her, she's just trying to get a rise out of you." When her eyes land back on mine, they are glistening with mirth, but all the same, she still mouths *stop it*, and gives me a funny look.

"Oh all right, if it's what you really want, I'll do you too." Shaking my head, I ready myself to stand while all three sets of eyes burn into my skull. Looking up with innocence plastered on my face, I say, "What? Did I go too far? Damn it, I did, didn't I? When should I have stopped? It was sloppy seconds, wasn't it? They never seem to like that one." I say the last part under my breath, as if talking to myself. "Maybe I should just set up an assembly line, work my way through y'all, what do ya think?" Planting my feet on the floor, I stand up, brushing my hands down the front of my jeans. "I've gotta go break the seal. You guys talk amongst yourselves, let me know what you decide." I navigate my way across the room and out the door to the bathroom, making sure to add an extra wiggle to my hips for good measure.

Chapter thirteen

Dan

"She's fucking with me again, isn't she?" Evan asks no one in particular.

With a nod of her head, Brianna confirms it. "Yes, Evan. She's fucking with you. She's not going to shag her way around the room. You can relax."

"I wasn't worried."

"Sure you weren't," she says, patting her hand on his chest playfully. Watching them together gives me hope that I might still have a chance with Cara. Her attraction to

Brianna is evident, but it seems that Bri has made her choice. Not to mention, Cara has been getting a little flirty with me.

It is time to up my game. Bring out the big guns, so to speak. "Is it getting warm in here?" Tugging at the hem of my top, I pull it over my head just as Cara is walking back into the room.

"Wooh! Get your gears off," she sings as she sashays her way over to me. "Check out the six pack on this one." Lifting my tee, she rubs her hand across my abs, and it takes everything to keep my cock from jumping to attention. "Seriously, there's not an ounce of fat on you, is there?" Her hand slaps down on my stomach before she covers me back up again, throwing her legs across my lap once more. Lifting my arm to throw it around her shoulders, she snuggles in to my side. "So, what'd I miss?"

Well that was certainly easier than I expected it to be. Should've taken my top off earlier.

"Nothing much, just Evan wondering if you were serious about your offer to do the rounds." With her in my arms, I feel like I can be more bold. My fingers find their way under her top, gently caressing her velvety skin as I relax further into the couch. Her soft curls tickle the side of my face as I lean into her, my lips brushing along her ear. "Personally, I don't think he could handle you."

When she raises her eyes to meet mine, her bottom lip pulled between her teeth, I can tell she is considering my words. "And you, cowboy? You think you can handle me?" She quirks an eyebrow, her lips pursed as she watches me.

She is so close it would be easy to kiss her. That thought alone has my heart racing, and all the moisture in my mouth seems to have evacuated, leaving me with the worst case of cotton-mouth I've ever had. "Uh… yeah," I croak, running my tongue along my gums, trying to regain my composure. *Pull yourself together, man!* "Of course. I can handle anything you throw my way." *Better.*

"Is that right?" Her tongue darts out, wetting her lips as she smirks at me.

"Ah, get-a-room!" Evan coughs the words into his fist and just like that, Cara turns away from me, poking her tongue out at him. *Damn, so close.*

"Aw, don't be jealous," she coos, her lips pushed into a pout as she gives him puppy-dog eyes.

"Jealous? Me? Pfft, what do I have to be jealous of?" Evan folds his arms across his chest, puffing it out proudly.

She hooks her thumb back towards me. "Have you seen him? He's like an Adonis, and you…" She trails off, tilting her head as she appraises him. "You're kinda… what's the word I'm looking for?" Her mouth twists to the side, her brow furrowed.

"Masculine? Handsome? Drop-dead-gorgeous, perhaps?" Evan throws the words out there with a chuckle and a wink at Bri.

"Nope, that's not it… I mean, you're easy on the eye, that's for sure, but it's more in the adorable, teddy-bear type of good-looking, not the Greek God type like my boy here."

I watch with a grin as Evan's jaw hits the floor, but he's quick to bounce back.

"That hurts me, blondie, right here." He thumps his fist to his chest. "Good thing I've got all these furry layers to take the heat from your burn." And without a word of a lie, he grips his shirt and rips it open, cave-man style, baring his sculpted chest to the room.

I inwardly groan while Cara bounces up and down, giggling like a mad woman. "Yes! Embrace your inner bear, Ev!" With two fingers in her mouth, she lets out a shrill whistle. "You know, he might actually give you a run for your money. Did you see that? He went all Clark Kent/Superman on me." She turns to face me. "I think you need to bare all too." Her finger pushes against my chest.

"I would, but," I lower my voice to a whisper, "I don't think you could control yourself around all this hotness." I run my hand down my torso in much the same way as she had earlier.

She peers up at me with those beautiful fucking seas of blue, and with a lift of one perfectly shaped eyebrow, she says the sexiest thing I've ever heard in my life.

"I'll show you mine, if you show me yours."

Chapter fourteen

Cara

You should see the look on his face! I don't think I've ever seen eyebrows shoot up so high before, but like I said, boys are easy. I'll have him eating out of the palm of my hand in no time.

"Is that a promise?" His voice is husky and I'll admit, it's a huge turn-on knowing that I have that much power over him.

Placing my hand on my chest, I look at him with what I hope is a demure face. "Would I lie to you?"

"Um, hello? Have you forgotten you have company?" Brianna says, and I'm sure I can hear a touch of jealousy in her tone.

"Don't be like that. You can take yours off too," I say with a wink. "I'm pretty sure I can speak for everyone here when I say, we will happily accept you exposing yourself. Right boys?"

"Well I'm certainly not going to say no," Evan says with a grin. "Although, I'd much prefer to have a private showing. I'm not really one for sharing." He waggles his eyebrows at her and that delicious blush runs across her chest and into her face giving her a soft glow.

"Uh..." Her eyes flick to mine and I silently will her to say no. "Yeah... maybe we should take this to my room?" Her voice goes higher as if she's unsure.

"Would you look at that?" Evan's shit-eating grin is spread across his face as he turns to look at me. "I guess some chicks dig the cute teddy-bear look."

With my hands in the air, I shake my head. "Hey, man, each to their own and all that jazz." I meet Brianna's gaze as she climbs off his lap. "You two kids have fun now."

"I'm all about having fun." He gives her ass a playful swat as she walks through the door, then turns to us with a thumbs up. Brianna giggles and takes his hand, leading him down the hall and out of sight.

"You okay?" Dan asks.

"Me?" I point a finger to my chest. "Couldn't be better."

"You still wanna play?"

"You know what? I think I'd rather go check out your room." I swing my legs off his lap and grab myself another bourbon. "I bet you've got all kinds of kinky shit in there."

He chuckles, the sound so deep and sexy. He's exactly the kind of distraction I need to keep my mind off whatever is going on down the hall.

"Lead the way, tiger."

With my hand firmly engulfed in his, I follow him past Brianna's room, noting the soft music playing behind the door. I don't let myself think about what else is being 'played' in there.

"Here it is." He sweeps his hand out in front of him. "My humble abode."

I saunter through the door, taking in the manly décor. A signed test jersey is framed and hung on the wall directly opposite his bed, which I'm surprised to see is made, and tidily I might add. Various memorabilia are displayed on shelves, along with several books, which I assume by their names, are all about rugby players. His shoes are all lined up neatly along one wall, and nothing seems to be out of place. Neat-freak much?

"Niiiiiiice," I say, dragging out the 'I' as my eyes scan the room. "You're very… particular about things, aren't you?"

Running a hand through his hair he shrugs with a grin. "I like order. Mess distracts me."

"Remind me never to let you see the inside of my room." He would have a fit! I have a shoe box that is overflowing with shoes, too many clothes shoved into drawers that won't close, and a pile of 'can-get-another-day-out-of-them' clothes on my chair. I also very rarely make my bed, unless it's clean-sheet day. Hello world, clutter be thy name! I mean, honestly, who can be bothered with cleaning?

"I'm sure it's not that bad."

"Oh, you have no idea." I can't help but giggle at the thought of him stepping foot in my room. "So," I clap my hands, flinging myself onto the bed. "Whatever shall we do with ourselves?"

Chapter Fifteen

Dan

She's sprawled across my bed staring up at me with those damn come-hither eyes of hers, and it takes every ounce of my strength to stop myself from mounting her right here and now.

Instead, I walk my hands up the bed on either side of her, taking in every curve of her body. When I reach the part of her stomach that is exposed, I trail light kisses along her peach-coloured skin. She sucks in a deep breath, goosebumps feathering her creamy complexion. Her nipples are on full display through her thin top and it's only now I realise she isn't wearing a bra. How the fuck did I not notice that before? *You're off your game tonight, Danny boy.*

Tugging the flimsy fabric up to let them loose, my tongue darts out, getting my first taste of her. So fucking good. I pull the tight bud between my teeth, eliciting a moan from her as she drags her fingers through my hair, pulling me closer. "Dan," she croons, grinding her hips against my thigh, almost sending me over the edge. With a growl, I roll onto my back, bringing her to straddle me. "Ooh, a bit of cowgirl action, I'm down with that." She nips at my mouth before pushing against my chest to sit back. With her eyes locked on mine, she rocks back and forth as she pulls her top over her head, spinning it around in the air like a lasso. "Ride 'em, cowboy!" she cries out, flinging her top across the room.

My hands grip her hips as she continues to grind her pussy against my cock, and all I can think about is how much I want to bury myself deep inside her.

When she reaches up and tweaks her nipples between her fingers, her swollen lip pulled between her teeth, I very nearly come in my pants.

A thump from the next room makes her stop what she's doing. She twists her head round to stare at the wall, listening for sounds. My fingers press into her hips, urging her on. "I'm sure everything is fine."

"Yeah, you're probably right." She turns back to me, her hips picking up where they had left off, but I can see the light has gone from her eyes. She's just going through the motions now.

As much as I'd like to make her forget all about Bri, I know I have to let her go. With a sigh, I drop my hands. "Cara, stop. We don't have to do this if you don't want to."

She cocks her head to the side. "I do want to…" Peering back over her shoulder, she raises an eyebrow. "I just need to know that she's okay."

I guess I should've seen this coming. I knew there was something more between them, but I let my other brain do the thinking tonight.

With a pat of my hands on her hips, she climbs off me, her eyes scanning the room for her top. I take in one final look at those beautiful tits, knowing I'll probably never get a chance to see them again after this.

Sitting on the edge of the bed, I watch her pull her top back on, surprised when she brushes her lips against mine. "Don't look at me like that, cowboy. I'll come back, I just need to check on her." She shrugs her shoulder. "She's my best friend."

Chapter sixteen

Brianna

Well that didn't exactly go as planned. What is wrong with me? Throwing myself at Evan like that. I'm acting just like... well, Cara. It's absolutely the sort of thing she would do.

Ugh! She went and got me all mixed up and confused. I have no idea if I'm coming or going, but I *do* know this; I won't be *coming* with Evan tonight, that's for sure.

Flopping back onto the mattress, I stare at the wall, wondering how it's possible to go from thinking I'm straight, to wondering what it would be like to have Cara in my arms. When I picture her tongue raking along her plump lips, I can't help but let out a tiny moan as I imagine those lips trailing over my body. What would it feel like to have her face buried between my thighs? To have her tongue lapping at my clit?

God, what am I doing? I'm fantasising about my best friend when she's probably next door shagging Dan's brains out. *Get a grip, Bri.*

Dragging myself off the bed, I creep to my door and slip down the hall to get a glass of water. The door to Dan's room is closed, and I'm surprised at the pang of jealousy I feel when I hear the familiar sound of Cara's voice mingling with Dan's deeper cadence.

Pushing that feeling deep down inside, I make my way to the kitchen, ignoring the mess of bottles and cans all over the coffee table. Grabbing a glass down from the cupboard, I fill it with water and lean my back against the sink, allowing the cool water to trickle down my throat.

"Bri?" Cara's eyes land on mine as she steps through the door. "You okay?" If I wasn't paying attention, I might have missed her eyes darting down to rest on my nipples. I hadn't bothered throwing anything over my threadbare singlet and cotton panties before leaving my room, and it is a little on the chilly side. Who am I kidding? It's not the cool air that has them standing to attention, it's the look in Cara's eyes and the images of her tongue roaming my body that have my heart racing and my panties soaking.

Clearing my throat, I mumble, "Um, yeah, I'm fine." *Why does it feel like all the air has been sucked out of the room?*

"Where's Evan?" She steps closer. "Oh no, was he a dud in the sack?" She holds her pinkie finger in the air, letting it curl down with a grin.

Giggling, I place my glass on the bench behind me. "I wish. That, at least, I could explain."

Cocking her head to the side, she juts out her hip, one hand resting on it as she looks me over. "Anything I can help with?"

If only she knew...

I shrug, averting my eyes from her intense stare. No one has ever looked at me this way before. It's as if she can see my thoughts.

"Are you sure?" she whispers, dropping her hand and moving in closer.

"I... um..."

With her fingers under my chin, she lifts my face to meet her gaze. "He's gay, isn't he?" she says matter-of-factly and I can't stop the grin from spreading across my face.

"He's not gay," I assure her.

"So... why'd he leave then?" Her eyes bore into mine and there's no way I can hide it from her any longer.

"Because I asked him to," I whisper, swallowing back the words I really want to say.

Her eyes flick between my eyes and my lips, her thumb caressing my jaw. "Why?"

"Because..."

"Because?" She raises an eyebrow, the hint of a smile on her face.

"Because I couldn't stop thinking about you."

Chapter seventeen

Cara

Because I couldn't stop thinking about you.

Her words ignite a fire deep inside of me, and it takes every ounce of self-control I have not to plunge my tongue down her throat.

"Finally! She admits her undying love for me." I say, brushing a strand of hair behind her ear with a wink. "I've wanted you for so long."

"You have?" she asks, biting the corner of her lip.

"I have." Taking the last step in so that our bodies are now touching, I can't help but groan at the feel of her against me. Trailing my hand along her arm and up to cup her cheek, my eyes flick up to hers, silently asking for permission.

With a small nod, she closes her eyes, puckering her lips. I have imagined this very scenario so many times in the dead of night, wondering what her lips would feel like. My fingers have done a lot of walking to that vision—believe you me—but now that the moment is here, I'm a little scared. *What if she changes her mind?*

My heart almost beats out of my chest as I lean in slowly, brushing my lips lightly across hers, hesitantly. When she doesn't shy away, and a tiny sigh utters from her lips, my bravado returns, and darting my tongue out, I lick along her bottom lip. She quivers beneath my touch. Pressing my lips to hers with more force, she opens up to me, her tongue duelling with mine as our kiss deepens.

Trailing my hand down her neck and over her soft mounds, I find that nipple I'd spotted straining against her top as soon as I saw her standing in the moonlight. She's never looked more beautiful to me.

Pushing the fabric aside, I cup her breast in my hand, my thumb rubbing circles around her tightened bud, eliciting a moan from her. Letting my other hand run through her hair, I take hold, pulling gently, giving me access to her neck. Licking my way down to the rosy bud between my fingers, I take it in my mouth, my tongue flicking across the sensitive nub.

"Cara," she utters my name on a sigh. Her back arches as she braces herself against the kitchen counter. I can't stop myself, lowering to my knees, I kiss and lick my way down her body, my hands caressing her thighs as I gently coax them apart. When my fingers brush against her wet panties, I moan against her skin. Hooking my thumbs into the cotton fabric, I slowly ease them down her legs, my lips following. By the time I lick my way back up to her centre, she is shaking with need.

"God, you're so beautiful," I whisper, before flattening my tongue and licking from entrance to clit. "And a natural red-head too, it would seem."

A throaty chuckle bursts forth, making those delicious breasts of hers jiggle. What a sight!

"Like you didn't already know," she says, looking down at me from above.

"Well sure, I just didn't know if the carpet matched the drapes." Before she can come back with an answer, I dive back in, nipping at her clit.

"Fuck," she hisses, throwing her head back as her hips jolt forward. Her hands tighten their hold on the counter as she grinds her pussy against my mouth, begging me to give her what she craves. Hearing her come undone under my touch, there's no way I can deny her.

"Look at me while I fuck you with my tongue," I say with another quick flick against her clit. When she turns her smouldering gaze on me, I can feel how much she wants this.

Plunging my tongue between her folds, I grip onto her ass, holding her in place. She tastes even sweeter than I imagined, and the tiny mewls she makes has me reaching between my own thighs, my fingers bringing me quickly to the edge of ecstasy.

Taking her sensitive nub between my lips, I gently suck, rubbing my tongue back and forth, while dipping a finger between her slick folds. She's so wet.

With our eyes locked on each other, I draw my finger from inside her, and press it into my own soft flesh, intoxicated by the feel of our juices mingling. I moan against her clit, as I slide my hand up her stomach, towards her mouth. Without hesitation, her tongue darts out, licking our essence from my finger, sending a surge of heat to my core.

As she pulls me deep into her mouth, I increase the pressure of my tongue on her tightened bundle of nerves until she cries out.

"Oh my God, Cara! I'm gonna come!"

There is no sweeter sound than hearing those words fall from her lips. It's enough to send me over, my orgasm rushing through me with an intensity so fierce I can barely move. Bri rocks her hips against my face, pushing my tongue deeper as she finds her release at the same time. I lap up her sweet nectar, drawing her nub between my lips until her breathing subsides.

Peering up at her, I'm greeted with a sexy just-fucked smile.

"God, that was… amazing," she breathes.

With a mischievous grin, I cock my head to the side. "Who said we were done?"

Chapter Eighteen

Dan

Any guy in his right mind wouldn't be able to step away from the scene that had just unfolded before my eyes. Feeling worked up, I'd decided to go for a run to cool off, only to stumble across the hottest thing I've ever seen in my life; Cara on her knees with an almost naked Brianna riding her face.

Unable to drag my eyes away from my very own private porn show, I'd gripped my cock in my fist, slowly pumping away in the shadows, hoping like hell they didn't see me.

Knowing it was only a matter of time before they turned their eyes my way made it that much hotter.

When Bri cried out, *"I'm gonna come!"* it was my undoing. My hips thrust into my clenched fist until I felt the familiar tightening before blowing my load into my balled-up tee. I'd had to bite my tongue to stop myself from crying out.

With my tee now scrunched in my hand, and my cock hanging limply, I still can't seem to step away from the gap in the door. I'm transfixed by the two beauties before me.

Both coming down from their high, Cara grins up at Brianna, her face alight. They exchange a few words before she begins to kiss and lick back up Bri's body, lingering on her perky breasts, and my cock instantly jumps to attention once more.

With her fingers pulling and kneading at the soft flesh, Cara continues kissing up Bri's body, finishing with a long lick from the base of her throat to her ear. Bri gasps, her shoulders pulling up as she begins to giggle. It looks as though Cara is whispering in her ear, her emotions playing out on her face. Oh to be a fly on the wall so I could hear what crude things she is saying to make her blush like that.

And then, as if in slow motion, her eyes widen and simultaneously, they turn towards me, their eyes locking onto mine. Cara grins and wiggles her fingers in my direction while Brianna buries her face in her hands. I'm rooted to the spot like a deer in headlights, unsure whether to make a run for it or face the music as the perve I am.

"Uh…" I stutter. "Shit, sorry… I just…" I hook my thumb over my shoulder as if that somehow provides an adequate excuse for watching them make out. My fingers fly through my hair as I huff out a puff of breath resignedly. "That was fucking hot," I admit.

"Thought you'd like that." Cara grins, her eyes flickering with amusement.

"You knew I was watching?"

She nods, cupping her hand beside her mouth. "Yeah, not quite as stealthy as you thought. I've gotta say," she shakes her head, "I'm a little disappointed. For a sportsman, you're not very light on your feet."

"I'll try to be quieter next time." I chuckle and Brianna groans behind her hands.

"I'm so embarrassed," she hisses.

Ashamed that my presence has made her feel this way, I take a step into the room. "Bri, trust me, you have nothing to be embarrassed about. That was hot as hell."

She peels her hands away from her face. "Really?"

"I wouldn't be standing here with my dick in my hands if it wasn't."

"Oh." A shy grin pulls at her lips and her blush deepens. Her eyes drop to the floor as Cara leans in, brushing her lips along her jawline and up to her ear. Bri draws the corner of her lip between her teeth, as she bobs her head in a small nod.

I don't know whether to stay or leave them to it, but before I can make my mind up, Cara turns to me with a quirk of an eyebrow.

"What do ya say, cowboy? Feel like making a sandwich?"

Chapter Nineteen

Cara

Whoever said you can't have your cake and eat it too was a knob end. Who wants to have a cake you can't eat? I for one plan on devouring every little morsel I can. You never know when you'll get an opportunity like this again. I'm not about to waste what could be the one and only time I get to be with Bri.

The fact that she is willing to give it a go too is beyond hot. That tiny nod of her head telling me she trusts me to look after her in what promises to be the hottest fucking sandwich in the history of sandwiches is enough to get my juices flowing. Even if Dan is standing there with his mouth opening and closing like a fish out of water.

"You need me to clarify for ya, big boy?" I point a finger between the three of us making a triangle in the air. "You, me and Bri getting down and dirty. You game?"

"Holy fuck, you're serious?"

"Well, yeah. Unless you'd rather go back to your room and take matters into your own hands while you listen to us some more." I turn to Bri with amusement. "I mean, I'm totally fine with that scenario too." And there it is; that sexy blush. "But I thought that seeing as the two of you haven't partaken in a threesome before, I may as well pop your ménage cherry. Ya know, because I'm giving like that." I pull my hand into a fist and draw it into my chest, boyband style.

"Well when you put it that way..." He grins and gestures down to his tented shorts. "I mean, obviously, I'm in."

Yes! I want to clap my hands and give a round of high fives, but I restrain myself, instead taking them both by the hand and leading the way to Dan's room.

"So, ah, how does this work, exactly?" Bri asks as I close the door and shuck off my jeans.

"It's all about what feels good, baby." I wink and throw myself on the bed. They both stand there staring at me, I guess waiting for instructions. Patting the bed, I summon them to join me. "Seeing as this is your first rodeo, why don't we start off slow?" I gently push Brianna until she is lying on her back, her eyes trained on me. Brushing soft kisses along her neck, I run my hand up from her waist until I reach those perfect fleshy mounds. With my finger and thumb, I pinch the puckered bud, my palm kneading her flesh as I lick a trail down to meet them.

Dan's hands roam my body, gently exploring every curve as he licks and nips at the base of my neck, making me shiver. I moan, arching my back and pressing my ass into his hard cock.

When I feel the feather-soft touch of Brianna's hand running up my arm, her fingertips brushing the side of my breast, my whole body tingles with anticipation. Rolling onto my back, I place her hand on me, showing her how to touch me just right, while my lips seek out Dan's. With one hand gripping him firmly, sliding up and down his impressive length, my other slips down to Bri's already soaking pussy. In some sort of kinky production line, I co-ordinate my fingers to slide in and out, back and forth, bringing them both to a frenzy.

Brianna's nimble fingers seem to be getting the hang of things as she kneads and sucks at my breasts, tentatively making her way down my body, where Dan has taken up residence. His meaty fingers plunge deep into my core, matching me stroke for stroke.

When he withdraws from me and all I can feel is the hot breath of Brianna on my clit, I whimper, begging for more.

"I... I don't know what to do..." she whispers.

"Here, let me show you." Dan slides down my body, parting my legs. "Fuck," he mutters as he takes in the groomed arrow pointing to the fun park.

Bringing my hands up behind my head so I can get a better angle on the two of them, I grin, shaking my ass side-to-side. "Ya like? I almost went for the vajazzle but thought an arrow pointing to the goods was really all that was needed."

"I like it," Bri says, her tongue darting out to lick around the edge, and I very nearly knock her out as my hips jolt upwards at the touch of her lips.

"Good," Dan says, his voice husky. "Now do the same thing with your tongue, but do it here." He traces a finger from the tip of the arrow straight down to my clit.

"Like this?" she whispers before diving in, her tongue flicking softly. I have wanted this for so long that I have to fight to keep my hips from thrusting against her face again.

"Mmmm."

"Now try this." He nudges her aside, plunging his tongue into my entrance, his thumb circling my clit a few times before he pulls away. "Your turn." He shifts back onto the bed, crawling up towards my face as Brianna sinks her tongue into me, her excitement evident as she laps and sucks like a pro.

Taking Dan's cock in my hand, I give it a few pumps before coaxing him to straddle my chest so I can take him in my mouth.

"Oh, fuck," he hisses, as I swirl my tongue around his swollen head. His hand finds the back of my head as he thrusts his hips, begging for my mouth.

"Steady there, cowboy, you don't wanna blow your load before we even get started." Securing one hand firmly around his length, I slowly pump as my lips slide around him, taking him to the back of my throat.

"Shit that feels good."

"Umhmmmm," I hum against him. It does feel fucking good. Brianna has mastered the art of cunnilingus, now adding her fingers into the mix and it's getting harder to keep my lower half still. God, how I want to ride her face. The only thing that would make this hotter is if I could watch her at the same time. In fact, that's a bloody fantastic idea.

I pull back, my lips slapping together with a pop as his cock bounces in front of me. "You know, you make a better door than a window." I nod my head to the side, letting him know where I want him. He obeys, kneeling beside my head instead. I twist my body so that I can watch Brianna and still get a mouthful of Dan.

Locking eyes with Bri, the intensity of her lips on… well… mine, suddenly kicks up a notch and I know I'm close. My hips start moving of their own accord and she wraps her arms around my thighs, holding me still while she increases the pace, her head thrashing back and forth.

I can't hold it back any longer, throwing my head back I cry out, "Fuck!" as she brings me to an overwhelming high. Her tongue relentlessly laps up every last drop until my body relaxes.

When she finally lifts her head, she wipes her mouth on the back of her hand. "Mmmm."

"Are you sure you're not a closet lesbian?" I ask with a grin.

"I think I could be persuaded..." *Holy fucking shit! Did she just say what I think she did?*

Chapter Twenty

Dan

Watching these two make eyes at each other reminds me that I'm the third wheel in this equation. Once again I'm left watching these two beauties with my dick in my hand, off to the side like some sort of creep. All I need is a moustache and those tinted aviators to have the full effect.

Part of me feels as though I should back out and leave them to it, but the other part of me, the one that isn't looking forward to a case of blue balls, is really wanting to get to the finish line.

Cara's tiny hand still grips my cock, pumping slowly while she eye-fucks Brianna. I've never done anything like this before, so I don't know the correct etiquette, but I'm pretty sure blowing my load across her face while she's locked in an eyegasm isn't appropriate.

Eyegasm. The chuckle escapes my lips before I realise what I'm doing and both sets of eyes turn to mine.

"Something funny, Danny boy?" Cara smirks, amused by my faux pas.

I open my mouth to say something but her hand picks up the pace, and the words no longer seem important. Without batting an eye, she reaches down, cupping Brianna's face in her palm. "Get your ass up here."

With a giggle, Bri crawls seductively up the bed until she is lying alongside Cara, her fingers tracing circles over her luscious body while she nuzzles into the crook of her neck. She licks and nips her way up to Cara's mouth until she can't help but turn and smash their lips together. So fucking hot. I can't take my eyes off them as their tongues war with each other.

I'm so close, my hips begin thrusting back and forth, matching her hand until she stops altogether, her warmth no longer surrounding me. Fuck!

"Don't you just hate when you're so close like that?" she asks with a wink and I have visions of tying her to the bed so I can finish the job. "Good thing I'm not done with you yet, huh?" She rolls so that she is on all fours, backing her tight ass up to me while she shuffles Bri further up the bed.

With a devilish grin over her shoulder, she raises an eyebrow. "Well? What are you waiting for?" She wiggles her ass in the air then lowers her face to Brianna's glistening pussy, giving me the perfect view. I don't need any more encouragement.

Placing my hand on her firm flesh, I tease my cock up and down her folds before plunging into her. Goddamn!

"So fucking tight," I mutter as my hips mimic a jackhammer, pounding into her in a steady rhythm. Reaching forward, I cup her breasts in my hands, kneading the delectable mounds with my palms.

When I pinch her nipples, she moans into Bri's pussy, causing her to rock her hips up on a whimper.

"That's it, right there," she moans, her fingers tangling in Cara's hair as she rides her face. With her lip pulled between her teeth and her red hair splayed across the pillow as she thrashes about, I can tell she is close.

With renewed determination, I snake my hand between Cara's thighs, finding the sensitive nub. Using my thumb, I tease circles first slow and then fast. Her walls start to shudder, milking me until I can't see straight. With a roar, I ram my hips into her, the sound of flesh on flesh echoing around the room, until like a deck of cards, we reach our highs one-by-one and then collapse into a heap.

"Best. Fucking. Sandwich. Ever."

Chapter Twenty-one

Bri

When I peel my eyes open to see that it wasn't all a dream and Cara is in fact curled into me, her soft breath brushing lightly against my neck, I can't help but smile at the memories of what we did last night.

Taking advantage of her sleeping so peacefully, I let my eyes drift over her body, taking in every beautiful curve. The same curves I kissed and licked as we pleasured each other through the night. Those soft breasts that pressed against me as our tongues lazily explored. And that goddamn arrow that pointed to her most sensitive spot.

Just thinking about everything we did has me panting, and my core throbbing. I have to press my thighs together to give myself some release, even if it's only brief.

"You know, if you keep squirming like that, I'm going to have to perform a mathematical equation on you." Cara grins up at me with a waggle of her eyebrows.

"I'm not sure I know what you mean," I say on a breath, biting my lip.

"Well, when a girl and a girl love each other very much…" she starts and her gaze turns heated.

"You love me?" I whisper.

"Yes. Is that okay?" Her voice is small and she suddenly looks vulnerable. I reach out to brush a strand of hair from her face. With her cheek cupped in my palm, I nod my head.

"I love you too," I admit. "I always did, but now…"

"It's weird huh? It's okay. You don't have to explain. I knew it was probably a one-time thing." She forces a smile on her face as she pushes herself up and swings her legs over the side of the bed.

Here goes nothing…

Curling my body around her, I slowly plant kisses from the curve of her back up to the base of her neck. Bringing my lips to her ear, I whisper, "Now, I think I love you more than before." I rest my chin on her shoulder and wait for her response.

She gives me the side-eye. "Are you saying you want a lifetime pass to the fun park?" She waves her hand up and down her body, wiggling her hips as she does.

I laugh, nodding my head.

"You sure? Because I have a no returns policy. And I'll need you to sign… on the arrow… with your tongue." She winks.

Climbing off the bed, I step in front of her, bracing my hands on her shoulders as I lower myself to the floor. Looking up at her, I lick my lips. "Never have I ever, been more sure of anything in my life."

A note from Cyan

I did it! My first attempt at writing smut is complete! I sincerely hope you enjoyed reading it because I have to say, I had an absolute blast writing something crass and out of my comfort zone. It was freeing!

I never would have had the courage to do this without the push of a good friend who shall remain nameless to keep my identity a secret. You know who you are! I love you, and I'm so glad you encouraged me!

Also to Spell Bound for their amazing proofreading skills. You guys rock!

And the lovely Mal at Inked Imprints for designing my kickass cover! Love you woman!

www.ingramcontent.com/pod-product-compliance
Ingram Content Group UK Ltd.
Pitfield, Milton Keynes, MK11 3LW, UK
UKHW020215250726
13967UKWH00001B/1 9 780473 395605